Feb 11, 2 '13

Dear Carol,
I did
to thank you for the
enormity of your gift.
Immediately I thought of
the little drummer boy.
He knew what to do!
I did cry upon receiving
all the books and people
tell me they cry when
they read these books
They are all "tears of
Joy"
Thank you so very,
very much.
Lovingly,
Regennia Risker

Bette Regennia Rinker

Bombs & Magnolias
If I Ever Make It Home Again

RoseDog Books
PITTSBURGH, PENNSYLVANIA 15222

ISBN: 978-1-4349-8389-3
eISBN: 978-1-4349-4638-6

Printed in the United States of America

First Printing

For more information or to order additional books,
please contact:
RoseDog Books
701 Smithfield Street
Pittsburgh, Pennsylvania 15222
U.S.A.
1-800-834-1803
www.rosedogbookstore.com

Johnny

Sometimes he caresses the milky wave with his breath and, as he does, he breathes movement into his hands. Reaching forth into the heavens, he thinks it's time to gather that star for Georgia...No! a handful of stars. Then, stepping back into the void he gently throws them forth to where they want to land or where they need to land. There appears a twinkle in his eyes at his and Georgia's creation...triumphantly satisfied with their forever...in this their timeless moment. He whispers "thank you" to God and, "Thank Georgia, for my brimming saucerful that is our tomorrow in time...our brimming saucerful of stars!"

Love comes finally
   drops about me
      on me
         in its way.
What did I know,
   thinking myself
      able to go alone
        all the way?
I was alone
   as a shadow to a rock
      and life heeded not my existence,
        but you came along.
And wherever I look
   I behold you
      and the secrets of life
        reflect in your eyes.

Acknowledgments

My greatest gratitude is for Georgia's excitement and willingness to share this piece of history and of her heart with me. Also, for Paul A. Diedrich, their son, who faithfully drove her to my salon regularly to add to her beauty and to write this true story.

Of course, we always drag our families into anything we do, so this is our "thank you" and dedication of this book to Johnny's bloodline and mine.

Edited by Daniel G. Diedrich
Cover by John Christian Jaksha
Computer Help: Matthew Joseph Jaksha
Georgia and John's family: Jon, Dan, Tad, Gigi, Paul
Grandchildren: Jeff, James, Julie, Joey, Jonathan, Jordan, Jenna, Nate, Daniel, Ted, Ben, Kate, Erin
Great Grandchildren: Kayleigh, Ana Jorga, Ava, Ian, Elija, Elle Jo, Cal

Regennia's family:
Matthew Joseph Jaksha
Kirsten and Kelly Dow; Colton and Kaden
John Christian and Judy Jaksha; Jewel, Joy

Why I Wrote This Story

This past year I have had the exceptional honor to meet and write about a remarkable family. A family with a dream and the courage to match all they believed in. This is the true story of one American hero whose grandparents migrated to America so they could have the rights and privilege of a dream.

Their dream was not just about self, but a dream that covers you and me every day in every way as long as we are right... morally right.

This one soldier made an effort that cannot be measured. We have made an effort to give you an account...a heavenly measurement of this one American hero's story.

His village of Avon, Minnesota can bask in Johnny's hard-won nobility, courage, and valor. It reminded me of Elijah in the Bible, who was complaining to the Lord how tired he was of fighting for the right all alone. But, God assured him that there were thousands more Elijah knew nothing about.

If you ever believe you are alone in fighting for what is right; it is our hope you will remember this account of one American hero who was admired for his bravery and noble deeds in all humility and care. We pass this true story on to you, friend, with the personal assistance of his loving soulmate, Georgia.

It's my belief that you cannot read this account without becoming a better person, as I have done.

This is my thank you to Johnny Diedrich, his family, and his fellow soldiers—who are ready and willing to go out in the fields of war so that you and I might be free. Thank you, Johnny! Thank you Fellow Soldiers!

Name: Diedrich

Vorname: Elmer Jo hn

Dienstgrad: Sgt.

Erk.-Marke: 4047   OFLAG LUFT 3.

Serv.-Nr.: 37 555 539

Nationalität: U. S. A.

Baracke:

Raum:

R. Lichly, Bayeu

E JOHN DIEDRICH
S SGT USAAF
WORLD WAR II
AUG 17 1922 ✝ FEB 29 2000
GEORGIA SCHMID DIEDRICH
1925

Georgia Veronica Schmid
Year Book Photo

At Johnny's request she sent this picture to him in Stalag Luft III. He carried this photo in the window of his billfold for the rest of his life....fifty five years.

Eulogy for E. John Diedrich, Jr.

June 17, 2000
Avon, Minnesota

by Daniel G. Diedrich

We have gathered here today to lay to rest my father, E. John Diedrich, Jr., in Avon, just down the street from the house where he grew up.

He had an adventurous and full life.

He would want us to remember that he fought in World War II to help keep the world free, but he wouldn't tell us that he was a hero. His sons who were bankers will remember his long and impressive banking career in which he rose from teller to CEO of a statewide banking corporation, but he never bragged about the details or what he had.

He would want us to remember that he graduated from St. John's University, but he never said much about the fact that he finished in three years and hit a grand slam for the Johnnie's baseball team in 1947.

He let his actions teach us the lessons he wanted to share about courage and humility, about persistence and integrity, and about commitment and joy.

But most importantly, he taught us through hundreds of small gestures and hand made gifts, and hugs and kisses, and at the end by the light in his eyes, that love was what mattered the most.

We won't forget your journey. This is our opportunity to say to you one last time, Dad, THANKS.

The Dream

After seeing my father alive for the last time during a Christmas visit in the year 1999, I had a dream that frightened me, but it was a beautiful and powerful and calming vision, as well. In the dream, my father and I were staying in a house high on a hill in the Southwest. There were stone tiles on the floors and the cactuses in the sun room on the back of the house were blooming. My father asked me to take him in his wheel chair out beyond the sun porch so he could gaze upon the valley below. Instead of the usual stark and dry vista of beige plateaus and blue mountains on the far horizon, we were mesmerized by lush green valleys and the verdant foliage that you would see in Ireland. There were a hundred different shades of green. Dark purple and grey storm clouds were swirling in off the Atlantic. We sat for a long time, entranced by the landscape.

Then I turned my father's wheel chair back toward the house and weaved a path through the dry cactus garden. Just as we reached the door, he said, "I want to go back, Danny." We turned around and wended our way back to the edge of the garden. As we looked out again over the gloomy cloudscape with the lush hills below, a bright window of light framed by even darker clouds opened up, so close to us that my father reached up as if to touch the window. I picked him up in my arms and lifted him toward the light as he continued to stretch his fingers closer and closer...

I thought that the dream meant that he was dying. After I called my mother, however, this proved not to be the case. But it remains a powerful image I have in my heart that helps me to reconcile myself to the fact that my Dad is gone and won't ever return.

See front of book for Eulogy to Johnny by Regennia Rinker

Chapter One:

Johnny – Step One

It was the year of 1943.

This story opens up in John Diedrich's mind, during World War II. There were shots flying all around them. They were at war with the Germans—over them, bombing England, Poland, and other European countries.

Fear could almost be seen and could certainly be heard. Absolutely nothing was reasonable anymore. Everyone's lot in life was set here at this exact point.

Nothing was understood except this one thing: One of the seven gunners in the B24 (of the head gunner, John Diedrich's plane,) had just given up. It didn't take one bit of nerve to inform John Diedrich that Bonner couldn't go back down in that hellhole ball turret. Bonner looked Johnny straight in the eyes with ghastly fear and shouted, "I will not and I cannot go back down there, sir!" Johnny looked at the gunner. Johnny could tell he was no longer in there. Where had Bonner gone? It seemed he had retreated somewhere into the recesses of his mind...just like they would have to do to survive this hell. It seemed like they were victims caught in between two worlds, with unfinished business, unlearned lessons, and dilemmas impossible to extricate themselves from.

Somewhere in here, the trap switched from the Germans to the gunner. Johnny didn't seem to have those mind-boggling traps. He couldn't wait to join this war as soon as he could. He simply wanted to make it stop; get it over with for himself and his village back home—which was passing through his mind. The memories were flooding and overtaking what the gunner was saying now. For an instant his mind reverted back home to the states and to Georgia. He knew his mind had been fully prepared by his little town of Avon, Minnesota; his church, St. Benedict; and his wonderful memories.

Village and home were really tops in Johnny's world. He didn't have to wonder and search feverishly for what he believed in. He often wondered why. He studied it a lot. Why him? Why didn't he have to ponder? Well, he did wonder about his town back home, which held something that was close to his heart.

In that crushing moment, his mind went back to the last time he was home. A nice lady, Mrs. Schmid, who he had run into at Avon Bank, just casually and sweetly invited him to their home for dinner the night before he was to leave for Langley Field, and then goes on to Italy. Johnny was in uniform and was in an especially good mood, as he had come to cash his service pay.

"Sure," he told her. "What time, Mrs. Schmid"? That was the least he could do, as the Schmid's owned the bank. After all, it was the Avon State that had given his father a position as head cashier—one of the opportunities they had moved to America for.

He knew but he hoped that his troop could not guess that underneath his veneer of strength, fortitude, and honor was a little boy from a small village that was built on a dream of immigrants; immigrants that had the courage to pull away from poverty and oppression in Germany. The courage to believe their children could have a better future than that.

On Furlough
First Date

Johnny
Determined to get the war over!

Nearly twenty years later, their own son now had to defend their dreams, which had catapulted them from their original home base in Germany to the good old United States of America...land of the free.

A young man dreams, too, and he had met the girl of his dreams that evening during dinner in the Schmid's home. Georgia had grown up...just plain blossomed. He could still see her clearly. He could see his home too. He knew it was there that he had learned how to be a fighter for what was good and right. First for his country, then his community, and then, of course, himself.

It looked like he would never see any of them again. There was no softness left here to hold onto except the desire to see everyone again.

So, despite the desperate struggle, Johnny was going to give it all he had. Through all this, Johnny managed to hold onto himself and all that he held dear.

He knew and understood full well that it was only he, God, and the pilot now. Even Bonner, his gunner, had let him down. He hoped that back home his church's doors were open...wide open.

Taking a deep breath he hoped his family and friends were there praying for him and this gall-darn war, because the flames of evil were as close as they could get right now. But, he understood there was only one thing that was going to save him and his crew and that was their Creator.

He made the sign of the cross on his chest which he knew would draw Jesus near. He understood that Christ embodied compassion, and that was just what he had to do. So, he didn't mind climbing down into the lower ball turret that was Bonner's position. His mind flashed back. Little did Georgia and her mother realize that when he accepted that dinner invitation to their warm and beautiful home the night before being shipped out, he had wanted to go because he liked that family and admired them. But, he also had the desire to gather up thoughts and impressions about why he was fighting. Why does anyone want to fight, he thought? Why does anyone want to rob the next person's rights away like a thief in the night?

For some reason, Bonner had placed a small ladder with seven steps on it going down into his lower ball turret. Johnny took a quick look at it and, without hesitation, told Bonner to take over his own position in the top turret (which is usually the head gunner's position) and he would replace Bonner in the pit.

Bullets were whizzing all around; ricocheting off the plane. Bonner, without hesitation, assumed the top turret (Johnny's usual position). No one saw Bonner pray. There was only one person that could help, and Johnny knew who that was. He was glad he knew his Creator.

On the first step he took, he realized he could shut out this horrific war. Just the way a banker would trade in securities or property for money. He could trade or hold onto his memories for survival.

There were sweet memories he could tap into. His fondest and most vivid were the night of the dinner party at Georgia's home. Right now this moment they were reflected back to him more powerfully than the small bombs exploding all around the B24 and the bullets that were dancing off the sides and wings. It sure wasn't a classical dance either. (He later touched and counted each hole on his last mission; there were over one hundred. He was amazed that he was still here to be able to do that.)

She was a tall, slender beauty with golden hair who studied the classics in the college of literature and music; who played piano and cello like an angel; who when she touched him could make the world stand still. Georgia was not only the prettiest girl in town, but she was the smartest—with a lot of talent to boot. She was the drum majorette for the Tech High band, and she had marched herself right into his head and heart.

Her beauty was inside and out. He learned that when he took her to the Paramount movies in St. Cloud. He discovered she had all the qualities a man likes. Oh, how she could play that piano. She played for local events and was invited to play for other cities. But the thing he loved most about Georgia was her spirituality. In fact, she and her family attended his church, St. Benedict. How lucky could he be?

It seemed all his buddies wanted to date Georgia, even guys just visiting town. All they had to do was meet her. Her sweet and innocent spirit just confidently showed itself freely. In fact, he always believed that she was a little above him.

Well she was every man's dream…making and loving peace. She sure stood out, then. It loomed large in his mind about how grateful he was to know her and her family. It was as though he had something to live for and to die for. What a lucky man he realized he was after looking upon the desperate and lonely man who seemed to have nothing to hold onto. *Yes, I'll take Bonner's place and I'll be glad I can do it!* he thought.

As Johnny stepped down to that first step, he knew he was going to hold Georgia closer than he had ever dared to hold her back home. It was odd that he didn't even hear the bullets whizzing by his plane—his dark plane now. Johnny wondered if his thoughts and prayers would ricochet back home—especially to Georgia, whom he was sure he would never get to see again. As the danger was so desperately great, it was a moment when dreams had to carry one into the next breath.

But he was resolved at all cost to try to get back home to see her and his family again. He didn't have to wonder why he had left though. He was determined that if he never did get to see all that he loved and cherished back in Avon; he would do all he could to stop the enemy. He was doggedly resolved to make sure he had left nothing undone in order to stop the aggressor—who seemed to want to rob his American dream—everything he treasured. *My thoughts may be abstract right about now, but this war sure isn't,* he thought.

Chapter Two:

Johnny – Step Two

He turned his head to make sure Bonner had moved into the top ball turret. He certainly didn't blame Bonner for not wanting to take the lower turret. He knew the blame went squarely on the aggressor, who was acting like a thief and willing to take what someone else had sacrificed and worked hard for. Avon (his village) never would hold thieves like that. They would have been run out of town promptly, with assistance.

Johnny realized he had only a few minutes to comprehend why he was taking the petrified gunner's place.

As he placed his left foot on the second step, his mind was racing now…the step seemed to move away from him as he searched for a chain of reasoning deep inside his soul. It was always home that evolved…will I ever make it home again?

Everything else seemed to be normal as far as war goes. His captain came to mind. He knew him as being tough, but thanked God he had trained his crew to be tougher. He remembered being put through drills that he thought no human should have to endure. But now he realized his captain was right, even more than right, because it meant life or death for Johnny and for America.

He loved the good ol' American way. He didn't have to stretch his mind at all to remember that wonderful German pot roast, with vivid orange carrots, onions and cabbage laying neatly around it at Georgia's home just a few weeks ago. He grinned remembering how sweet she looked. He could still see her little sister, giggling across the table from him as though she had a secret. He could almost taste and smell that delicious pot roast now. He could almost smell it, but Georgia smelled better than that. He wondered what kind of perfume she had on that night (roses, magnolia, or what)? *What more could a man ask for?* he thought. It seemed her family actually owned Avon. He could see so clearly that beautiful satiny blue suit she had on and a rather small pin that resembled a magnolia flower. After the dinner they sat in her parlor. He wished he had the nerve to ask her to play "*Georgia*" or "*The Star Spangled Banner*," but the classical music her mother had on all the time was nice, too. It was so soothing to hear as they ate and it helped me have nerve to ask Georgia to the movies.

Thank God I got that nerve, he thought. *I had never realized that the classics have such a profound effect on people.* He remembered how thrilled he was just to touch her. On the way home, she asked him to drop her off at the front door of her college. He did but he took her hands and asked her if she would write to him. She said "Yes." Consequently, that was the end of his furlough. The next day, he flew back to Langley Field, and then overseas to Foggia, Italy in his new home away from home, his B24.

Mrs. Schmid's home was just as beautiful as Georgia. It had all Queen Anne furnishings and Georgia in her obviously tailor-made suit.

Dang! he thought. Something flew into Johnny's eye… maybe mixed with a silent tear. Simultaneously, he flipped his body around and sort of leaned on the upper part of the ladder.

He then put his feet firmly on step two and three. He slipped off a glove from his right hand, which was hindering him from removing whatever it was stuck in his eye. He so wanted to believe it was a splinter.

For some reason he couldn't get Georgia off his mind. What was it about her that made it seem like he was still back home in her dining room? The chandelier, which was sparkling clean, and that pinkish-red rose on the dishes...that wonderful aroma coming through the door as he rang their doorbell, they all definitely meant so much more now... In his mind, he had rang that bell at least a hundred times or more before really noticing Georgia. *Ah yes, there's her mother with a big bright smile,* Johnny recalled. She hadn't bothered to take her apron off. *It seemed she welcomed me in like one of the family,* he thought. *In fact, I have never felt so at home... not even in my home.* He wondered why. He wondered what was happening to him...in all ways, deeper than those bullets flying all around him. Why were they not affecting him the way they were Bonner?

As staff sergeant, he looked around his plane. He was in charge. All eyes were on him. All he could think to tell them was to get the guns ready. He had purposely tried to not get close to the men under him because he knew it would be easier for them and him if a moment like this ever came.

Well it was here. He thought he heard a few of the soldiers mumble to another one, "The rotten plane's going down any minute and we're going to be blown to bits any second, and he's sitting there battling with a splinter!" (So they did think it was a splinter!!!)

But, that was Johnny's way. What his men would call defeat, Johnny would call just a splinter in the eye. Well, he could call this battle, his eighth one with the Germans, more of a twig or a thorn, but that was no reason to not put all your training to work to preserve God's will and country. He knew he had learned all he needed to know back home.

In Avon, the men were men and the girls were definitely ladies. No fine lines there. Therefore, each gender had a profound respect for the other. A respect that went on forever to Johnny. This moment seemed like forever. It wasn't that they were all alike in Avon; in fact, they were distinctively different, especially since Minnesota was referred to as the "melting pot" for immigrants. They seemed to be drawn to the ten thousand lakes, the uncountable trees—namely pine trees, and the kind of winters that many of them had left and were familiar with.

Winter was extremely hard in Minnesota. So much so that some of the residents would go south for those months and return in the spring with the birds.

For the families that stayed, Johnny would help shovel them out of terrible snowstorms. All the guys helped, they didn't want anyone to be unable to get to the doctors and the store for food. Naturally, this would build the guys muscles that lived there. They became nice and strong; much stronger than before. The girls noticed that. Little did Johnny know and would find out a little later what a valuable asset that would be for him in this war. As for the girls, he only wanted one to notice him. He thought she might have, but he was not sure.

He knew Georgia had noticed him some, but he wasn't sure whether she was just being polite or, maybe she had a passing interest in him. If she did, he wanted to show her just who Johnny Diedrich was when he got home.

Even a passing interest from the girl back home was good enough for Johnny then, as he flipped back over and continued on to step three.

Chapter Three:

Johnny – Step Three

What would he teach a girl that seemed to have it all? He certainly didn't want her to know or to have to ever experience this hell he was in at that moment. He hoped his crew had beautiful times and memories of home to help carry them through that torture...those times that try men's souls, as they were all experiencing at that moment.

What heroes they were in Johnny's eyes! He wasn't going to look them in the eye right now. He had to play it tougher than he had ever had to do in his short life, which he hoped would be longer.

No, I'll just think happy thoughts, he thought. It was the closest he could be to Georgia. Georgia and her two sisters were the happiest people he had ever known and he hoped they would never change or have to change.

The clang of constant bullets hitting his plane was an unchanging reminder of why he and his squad unit were there. Well, it was America's plane, but right now there was no difference. He understood full well he was that America. The America that his immigrant German grandparents wanted to be a part of in 1850, when Germany was Prussia. So much so that they packed up everything they owned and shipped it to America, migrating to the state of Minnesota. They left Germany because they didn't agree with Hitler.

They left everything they knew and loved in Germany to go build a new and wonderful life in a far away land called the United States of America. They had heard a lot about the states through gossip and letters, and also from the missionaries' work and radio programs.

If we get this plane back, will there be a letter or a card from Georgia? he wondered. It seemed too much to hope for a picture of her. He sure could use a picture of her right then.

Their families were so different, even though they were both of German descent. Maybe it made a difference that Georgia's family had actually owned the whole town...it seemed they had literally pioneered it. First, they started a lumber company there, then a bar. She had said when the babies began to come into the world, her Grandpa Schmid thought it better to sell the bar and build a bank. They acquired other parts of Avon. It was a place the local dignitaries would meet and court each other, in the guise of discussing local news. It was only an outward manner to hide the truth, and that always amused Georgia, even though people were somewhat proper in Avon...or maybe it was across the street from her grandpa's store...I'm not sure!

When the bank was built, Georgia's Dad was the one who sent for Johnny's Dad. The Diedrich's, were pretty well settled in southern California but didn't feel at home there. Then, the day that letter came. Mr. Schmid had invited them to come to Avon and be their head cashiers. Dad was happy. He didn't hesitate; he began to pack immediately and headed for a new future, full of peace and adventure for the asking in a land completely the opposite of where they were. There wouldn't be so many distractions. Johnny's father wanted out of the busy and crowded area. It was good; how glad Johnny was that his Dad understood that!

From the age of eight, Georgia was always involved with music. She was studying music at the St. Benedict College near her home. That made her perfect as the drum majorette for their band, as she understood beat and rhythm as well as anyone you will ever meet.

She played piano and cello for pretty much all the special events around Avon and surrounding towns. Johnny didn't think she would really be interested in him. *Why didn't I just break all the rules that last night at her college door? Maybe a kiss would have told me more,* he thought. *I did hold her hand and ask her to write to me when I get settled down somewhere.*

I wanted her to know that I knew she was a lady and also that I understood how to treat a lady, even though every fiber of my being wanted to hold her close, to kiss her, to tell her goodbye, and how very much I was going to miss her, he thought.

It took all his resolve and all his strength that he could muster up to refrain that night. It was then and now that it began to dawn on him how grateful he was that he had helped his family and their neighbors dig out from all those snowy, wintry, isolating snowstorms; the ones Minnesota is noted for. He knew somewhere in the back of his mind that was one of the things, among many others in his town, that had been conducive to his desire to do the right thing at all cost, even now… especially now.

I think, I hope, I conveyed to Georgia that I wanted to put her feelings first, Johnny thought, *that she knew, for a fact, that I so appreciated her being the lady she was. It did seem to me that she tried so sweetly to hide her feelings for me. How could I be sure?*

To Johnny, it seemed her look spoke of a war going on inside of her. Each time he had taken her hands, they were warmer than they should be. Both times at the movies and her college dorm they seemed full of fire. He liked that. Had he not been able to read her eyes, he probably would have never looked back… especially now!

But, Georgia was not going to give in to her feelings because Mrs. Schmid, her adoring mother, had taught her well to really know the man before you ever gave into or began to think about the word love, much less hugs and kisses. She felt there should be positively no intimacy outside commitment.

Johnny loved Georgia for that and he appreciated Mrs. Schmid for instilling moral values in her three daughters; plus the community concerns they were so conscientious about. Mostly, though, Georgia loved to entertain them.

If I ever get back home, I'll let them know what that meant to me and how very much it helped carry me through this war, Johnny thought.

Actually it had given him more courage than he ever realized he had to fight the aggressor, to preserve what his country's code of freedom stood for; not freedom to take what is not yours and rightfully earned, but the freedom to do what's right; not the freedom to do what's wrong. He hoped someday he would get the opportunity to teach his own kids.

He learned that guys were willing to die so that this code of honor might be protected. "My country tis of thee, sweet land of liberty" slipped into his mind and he couldn't help but wonder if his Mom, Georgia or anyone back home was praying for him in their little church of St. Benedict right now. His mom didn't make it to church as often as the Schmids and Georgia, but he went enough times for all of them. His mom would always beg off and say she didn't feel well, and she did have health problems…lots of problems! He could still cut across the tracks from his home put him in front of the parish. He could still slide in the side door just in time to smell the incense and to hear the choir in his mind. Georgia sat a little in front of him and she would always turn and smile shyly.

Johnny glanced around at his crew…he couldn't help but wonder what their families were like in the States. Did each of them or any of them have a girl like Georgia? He knew there was only one Georgia, but did they have a special someone they could carry in their mind to help them get through this hell?

He didn't want to admit it, but he could read in their faces that they didn't believe they would ever see home again. The fright, the awful sense of extremes...where does it end? The questions and terror that were on his men's faces were more than Johnny could bear. He heard words coming out of their mouths that he didn't really want to hear. So he looked down for step four.

The Church of Saint Benedict

Avon, MN 56310

— STAFF —

PASTOR
    Rev. James N. Reichert, O.S.B.

ORGANIST

CONTEMPORARY CHRISTIAN SINGERS
    Jeff Tromm

RELIGIOUS EDUCATION
    Connie Lacher, K-6
    Adult/Infant Initiation
    Geralyn Nathe-Evans, 7-12
    Youth Ministry

PARISH SECRETARY/BOOKKEEPER
    Joan Zwilling

— TELEPHONE —

Parish Office/Rectory 356-7121
Religious Education 356-7677
Kitchen 356-7769

— WORSHIP SCHEDULE —

WEEKEND MASSES
Saturday . . . . .5:00 p.m.
Sunday . . . . .8:00 a.m.
                                10:30 a.m.
WEEKDAY MASSES
Tuesday through Friday . . . . .8:00 a.m.
HOLY DAY MASSES
    Check the bulletin for schedule.
RECONCILIATION
Saturdays . . . . .4:00 p.m.

— REGISTRATION —

BAPTISM
    Baptism preparation - please call the Parish at least two months before the birth of your child.
MARRIAGE
    Arrangements must be made a minimum of three months in advance, six months preferred.
NEW PARISHIONERS
    We welcome you as a new member of our faith community. Anyone moving into the parish, please call the office at 356-7121 for an appointment to register.

Our parish church where we were married June 1, 1946. As children Johnny would slide in the side door late. Georgia would always turn and smile to him

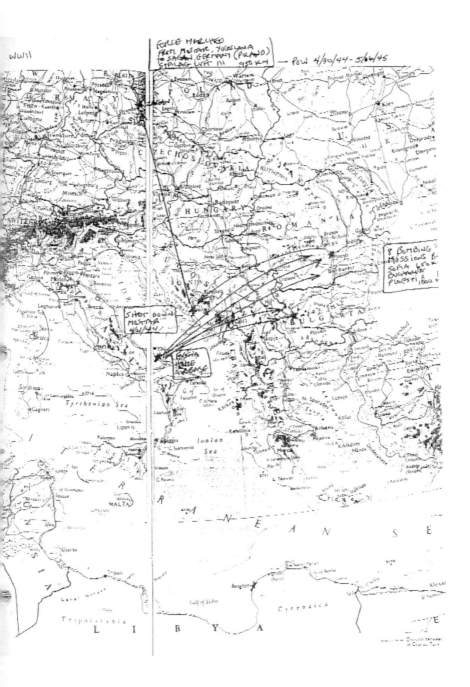

Johnny flew eight missions from Fogia, Italy to Polesti oil fields in Romania before being shot down.

Chapter Four:

Johnny – Step Four

Johnny knew one thing for sure; he knew and understood that this was going to be the hardest situation he would ever have to bear. It was getting harder to take the steps closer to the lower ball turret.

I'd better scope the crew before I take that position, he thought. Thank God he had never allowed himself to get too close to his crew. His training had taught him that this time may come. Could he look back? Could he bear the look on the men's faces? All he could think to say was, "Get your guns sighted, here we go!!!"

Well, it wasn't that bad. Bonner had kind of a half grin as if to say, "Thank you, sir for everything—especially for taking my place. I appreciate it sir!" It was also a grin that spoke of this hell. It was a grin of goodbye...fully believing that Johnny would be taken out in his place. He was so grateful to Johnny.

It was alright with Johnny, he knew he had been well trained and disciplined for this moment. *God those drills were hard*! He remembered.

Now he could really see the church back home. It above all was coming through loud and clear, almost like a last rite he had heard about. *Could this be it for me* he wondered. *That's okay. I'll take Bonner's place. I've trained hard and feel well prepared. I'm prayed up. I've got a girl back home that cares…that knows how to care and would be concerned about what happens to me. Yes, Georgia cares…that feels good to say. I hope and pray she does!*

Who knows what is going on in the universe the very moment your soul is on trial for life or for death? Little did head gunner John Diedrich know that back home, a few years earlier, the die was cast and little Georgia Schmid had fallen completely in love with him.

Little did he know, he had everything to live for. Little did he know that ahead of him was a love back home that would be returned and reciprocated beyond full measure and have the capacity to transcend space and time. It was as though "catch a falling star and put it in your pocket, never let it slip away" came humming through his mind with these thoughts. Oh, how he wished he could catch a star right about now and send it back home to Georgia.

After all, she did promise to write that night he took her to her college door. He wondered. Where she would ever send a letter to in the middle of the chaos? If he didn't get to pick it up, who would? Would it be like a "Dear John" letter, like some of the guys had gotten, or would there be a picture in it? The guys won't believe how beautiful she is. Some of the guys already had pictures of their grandmothers or moms out; nobody like Georgia was on display in their plane.

To fall in love with Georgia was not a whimsical thing. No, to fall in love with Georgia was nurturing one another's dreams; keeping the home fires burning; watching out for your neighbors, and then the country.

Ironically, Johnny had to turn that around by making sure the country was safe, then the village, then the dream.

Georgia knew she had always admired Johnny. In fact, her heart skipped a beat at the first sight of him. She remembered well that she was in the fourth grade when he was in the sixth grade. He seemed to be way out of her reach and never noticed her...didn't even look her way.

She remembered running upstairs of her home to look out her bedroom window if she thought he would be going by. Later on, they seemed to be caught up in preparing for life. They didn't really have time to think about what the other was doing too much then.

The only one that could perceive what her daughter's heart was doing was Mrs. Schmid, her mom. Yes, her mother could see the subtle changes slowly taking place in her oldest daughter in a more profound way than anyone else. She couldn't help but wonder why. She became more alerted about Georgia's changes and began to ask questions.

No one could tell Mrs. Schmid much, but she perceived that there had been born in Georgia a natural curiosity about that new cashier's son, who Georgia's father, George, had brought to town from southern California. Anyone she mentioned him to thought he was wonderful.

Mrs. Schmid kept her eye on things and tried to stay out of that part of her daughter's life. She tried to keep Georgia interested and active in her music, her grades...anything but boys.

On the other hand, she had heard from the residents of the little town that Johnny was kept very busy helping his parents with the many chores they had for him. In his spare time, she had heard from the men of the town that Johnny had taught himself to be an accomplished fisherman and hunter in the woods not far from his house.

Could you call it a home, he wondered, *if there was a good breeze with snow and rain coming in through the door cracks and windows?* Well, Abraham Lincoln did; so Johnny reckoned he could too. After all, it wasn't always going to be like that…this was America and if you worked hard it was guaranteed you would do well. Abe taught us that.

As he grew up, Georgia could see how he looked out for the older people in town when they asked for help. She so admired him for that. She saw more than Johnny knew. In fact, she had a firsthand view of just about everything Johnny did when he was in town.

When Georgia heard clink, clink, clink…she knew it was Johnny playing horseshoes with his boss and the guys at the garage after work. She would lay on her bed and lean out the window until Johnny made his way home at about ten after playing penny ante until bedtime. She could see him under the streetlights down the block…past the church and around the corner. She would watch until he disappeared; only then could she go to sleep. Before she fell asleep she would think, *He was a smart man to hire, Johnny Diedrich.*

As he grew up, Georgia could see also how he looked when the elders of the town would in their way and with their wisdom look after him. She so admired him for that. She saw more and knew more about him than he ever realized because of her upstairs window that looked out over the town her Grandpa had helped build.

Georgia saw from her window the first job Johnny was ever given at their local garage, which would pay for the Model T he had just bought from the local priest, considering that he had to keep gas in it.

He kept the black on it shining like a new nickel. His friends loved that car too! They loved to be seen in it with Johnny. So much so, they would pay him to chauffer them to wherever they needed to go.

Perhaps they knew Johnny could use the money…they understood that he was newer to town than their folks and had not had the time to be as well-established as their families were.

They also understood Johnny well enough to realize he would someday be just as proven as them. They could see the piercing eye he had for details, his love of the challenge in anything life threw at him, and, above all, as they continued to observe him they could see his great love and respect for life itself. In fact, they wanted that zest for life he had. They wanted to be just like their friend Johnny, whom they knew to be good at anything he touched.

Was it a gift he had, or was it something they could have also? They noticed Johnny was too busy to bother with girls but they would pay him to drive them over to Albany, which was about eight miles away, to take in a movie and drive around and check out the girls. They would pay Johnny's way, too!

Georgia was just as busy too. Her mother made sure she was practicing her scales on the piano and with her voice, in between her tap dancing lessons and twirling her baton for the band. She always led the band and usually led them into victory, achieving first place in state competition.

But it didn't mean life or death to Georgia, as she had been taught and disciplined to believe it's not whether you win or lose but how you play the game. In other words, winning had no value if you didn't play in a manner that would give value to all the players by being such a good sport.

In between all that, Georgia would squeeze time in to play the clarinet and cello, plus take breaks to swim, tap dance, roller skate, and ice skate.

But many of her breaks were taken up with helping in her Dad's variety store and helping her Mom with the cleaning and cooking. She especially loved to help her Mom and Dad in their garden. Her mother promised her it would pay off someday, and pay off it did with Georgia and Johnny. They had been skillfully prepared by their parents and their community to be cultured, to love and be able to articulate beautiful things. They were just as skillfully prepared to make wise decisions and commitments throughout their lives. Whatever was cultivated in them, they later would lovingly hand down through their entire families, village, and country. Their problems were worked on skillfully with team work.

Henceforth they noticed and admired the qualities of each other. They somehow comprehended that deeper than they were conscious of until years later, until that dream of what Johnny was defending materialized years later. But Johnny knew more than ever that if he ever got the chance again he was going to nurture that dream and put all of himself into it. Above all else, if a man can fight a war like this and put all of himself into it, he can do the same with his dream. *Easy*, he reasoned. *Yes, it would be first and the world would know* it. He knew then in his soul it could happen if he was right and with God's help. Reality began to set in. He looked out his plane's window and saw a stream of fire coming. Thank God he hadn't put his glove on yet! He had something to say. He pointed at the fire and said in his quiet manner "I'm telling you, bullets and bombs, if I ever get the chance I'll nurture my dreams…really nurture them with everything in me. Come hell or high water, bullets and bombs won't stop me".

The guys sort of looked at the head gunner and then one another but they understood this one thing, their leader was strong. They believed in him!

Georgia understood that also. Even though her years were tender, she knew it with all of her young heart. No one had observed Johnny Diedrich as close as she had. Add to that an unexpressed love and you have magic.

But because of the war and fighting constantly all around him, he knew well his dream was the nurturing of his home, his friends. But most of all it was that wonderful community of people in Avon that had made him ready for this war and someone like Georgia was, who was warm, loving, caring, and fully capable of keeping the home fires burning.

Georgia was all of those things. Just what any man wants and needs. She was fully prepared and qualified. In fact, she trained for her role in life every bit as hard as Johnny did for the war.

He was fully prepared and determined to protect her, our country, and many other lands from any aggressor that intends to rob, kill, and destroy. That's what the Bible says...the devil comes to rob, kill, and destroy—but not if we can do anything about it. Quicker now, he took the fifth step.

What exactly was it going to be? Johnny wondered. *Them or us?* Johnny knew he was prayed up and ready, but he understood that he had left a lot of things undone and unsaid back home. He knew also they were safe in his heart.

Flashing back to Avon...his hands were sweating and he could feel the blood rush to his neck and face. He could feel the touch of Georgia's hand. That was funny; he didn't usually sweat except that time he dared to take Georgia's hand for the first time in the theater and also at her college door when he told her goodbye. It was really a goodbye he hoped to never have to say again. In his mind, it was, "Just...so long for now."

Chapter Five:

Johnny – Step Five

The fifth step was closer. Georgia was closer in his mind, but there was no longer time for anticipation. He prayed there would be. There wasn't even time to spit. Thank God that darn splinter was gone…tearfully gone!!!

Johnny was a survivor. He knew that from going through the depression and that time he and his family had to live in an unfinished shack out by the Avon Lake, just on the edge of town.

There had been no running water or indoor plumbing. Johnny learned to do everything outdoors. His favorite thing to do on weekends when he didn't have to help his Dad clean the barn was to take off into the nearby woods to trap muskrat, mink, rabbits, and squirrels. His job at the gas station made the payment on his Model T and the trapping fun on weekends paid for the gas to keep it running.

Thank goodness, he thought back *that Dad shook me awake every morning at five to go stoke the fire at the bank.* Johnny would quickly splash the chilly cold water from Lake Avon on his young but not awakened face. Brrr!

That was enough to put a skip in his step and a whistle on his lips as he rounded the corner past the garage. As he went past Georgia's house, he'd always turn and look and think about that nice Schmid family. He remembered the time he knocked on their door and Mrs. Schmid came to greet him. He handed her a pail full of snapper fish. She said "Oh, thank you darling." That was the first time anyone had ever called him that. He wanted to get her all the fish in the lake for that.

He always looked forward to those dark early, mornings when it seemed like he owned the world. He loved this walk. He loved how the cold dark water felt on his young, sleepy skin. But, it didn't come close to how great Georgia's hand felt that night at the movies. These are the things he missed. He recalled how Georgia had taken her other soft warm hand and placed it over the top of his hand that was enveloping her other hand. This moment was the electromagnetic awakening of their love. But right here, right now this scene was worse than any movie he had ever seen. If only this movie could be over; if only he could be shaken by his Dad and told he was only dreaming; if only he could ask Georgia if she could remember what was playing at the movies when they first held hands…would she remember? But, he did remember almost skipping and whistling to the bank every dark morning. Some of the town's dogs would go with him to help. They didn't mind that every-one else was sleeping. He and that pack of dogs he called his friends, they seemed to understand the whole town of Avon depended on that bank being warm and ready for their daily business. Once in a while, the people would tell him so with a big smile and a "Thank you, young man" as they touched the top of his head. His Dad's words were ringing through his mind: "Easy now, son…hard later or hard now…and way easy later. Which one will it be?"

A lot of the things his Dad made him do, along with Sarg, seemed hard. But, it sure looked easy now—even the trapping, when some of those varmints seemed to outsmart him in their way. No matter what he did, they soon realized Johnny Diedrich wasn't going home without his full catch...no way! *So this is what hard really is!* Johnny thought. *That was a snap. This is hard.*

Johnny knew this war was the hardest thing he would ever have to deal with on this side of heaven. Thank God he hadn't been spoiled. He could tell which guys had been spoiled. He could tell by watching their faces and how each one mapped out their reality.

If this plane goes down, I know this much, I can survive by simply doing what has to be done. He thought. *Yeah, that's what my people in Avon taught me...just do what has to be done. Don't separate your life into work and play. Just realize it's all encompassed in this incomprehensible thing called life.* It was all making sense to him now.

After all, this was Johnny's eighth mission. But, he had never been sucked up into the ruptured bowel and boiling heat of action on the other seven...not as close as this. As he lowered into Bonner's place in the lower turret, he noticed his plane was still flying in its formations.

Chapter Six:

Johnny – Step Six

He was zeroing in on the sixth step almost reluctantly. He had one more to go…Oh, how he hated to take the seventh and last one into Bonner's place at that lower ball turret. The plane's altitude was still high, all that was left to do was aim the guns. He heard things he didn't want to hear come out of the other bombers mouths again and again, like "holy crap!" The plane began to descend to a lower position to drop its bombs. Abruptly, anti-aircraft guns began blasting them. The Messerschmidt fighter planes began to dive and fire directly at their home for now — the B24. Flame was bursting all around them. All hell had broken loose. Their engine had just taken a direct hit! Oh God it wasn't even turning. They were losing altitude rapidly.

The pilot yelled for Johnny to order everyone to bail out and fast. "We can't make it now over the Yugoslavian mountains…such a close refuge behind those mountains and we can't make it."

"Okay men you know the drill. Who yelled that?" No one knew anymore. Johnny had to push some out of the plane. They weren't ready to give up! Johnny said "We'll drop all over the place down there, but make those mountains your goal." He wished he had taken time to use the latrine but it was too late. It was too late for that seventh step he so dreaded. It was too late to even dream of kissing Georgia even though he knew he had her hand in his at that moment, like before. It was fifteen miles from home and he could barely see through the white fog and slanting rainstorm that beat on his old Model T's windows. No, wait a minute Georgia's Dad let us take his brand new Chrysler. The storm was a problem. He was so grateful that Georgia didn't complain. He was happy about that. He remembered thinking she'd make a great soldier! What a lady!!! She never said a word as though she wasn't there but he could feel her presence strongly. She was always there in a way.

Johnny reached over for her to let her know everything would be alright even though it seemed their whole world was filled with lightening and roaring thunder. That night, it seemed the whole world was feeling the electricity of their new-found undiscovered love. It came to him that at that college door when he had taken Georgia's hand and asked if she would write to him she said "Yes" loud and clear without having to think about it. That was a good sign.

That next day, leaving for Langley Field to fly out to Italy by way of Brazil and Africa was really almost as hard as this, but with a promise. He smiled…that made her a soldier's dream. She was kind of a dream within a dream.

Georgia, God love her, made it a lot easier by saying "Yes." Sometimes he would say "Yes" right out loud to remind himself of what she said. He did not want to leave Georgia in any way but by now bullets and thoughts were mixing so rapidly that only thoughts of surviving were emerging now.

He could hear the pilot yell over and over again "Bail out! Bail out! Bail out!" Johnny had honed his sense of timing many many moons back in Minnesota on those cold dark trapping nights. That keen sense kicked in. He knew this was an emergency. The plane was going to blow up any minute, so he began to push a couple of the gunners out. Each looking at the other in a last goodbye stare…a horror stricken stare.

Johnny was counting heads as rapidly as he could. He had long since hopped off step six. One gunner was missing; he thought it was Bonner. He looked around full circle. What's he laying there for? Johnny went over to lift him up. Those blankety-blanks had shot his head off. *Bonner was no more but they were gunning for me, the head gunner!* Johnny agonized. *Why did Bonner have to trade places? Why couldn't it have been me?*

"I'll make it right, Bonner," he told him as he lifted his lifeless body and body parts so that he could push him out. But first, he took his tags and wrapped them in a little piece of paper and put them in his own pocket to send back home. Before he pulled the rip cord, he made the sign of the cross and gave Bonner a good push, as he told him, "Godspeed, man. May you find a decent resting place." There was a lot more he wanted to talk over with Bonner. *Oh well, maybe we'll get our time for that in eternity*, he thought. As far as he knew, Bonner was a good man. He yelled after him, "There won't be war in heaven, the good book says." If they could only catch a glimpse of that promise, he knew heaven would begin right there, right then for everyone.

"Jump man, jump!" resounded in his ears.

It didn't matter any more that this was an American hero, an American warrior, a man with a dream, a man that had already risked his life several times for his plane. The plane burst into flames. Everyone was out but he and that crazy pilot that had wanted him to jump first so he could make sure Bonner's chute opened. In that moment the last bombing run flashed through his mind, when he literally had to walk out on the catwalk to release the bombs by hand. After that, he being the head gunner and had to literally lean out of a bullet riddled window and photograph the results of the bombing for Washington.

They lost altitude. The plane was on fire. There was fire under him. He calmed himself by going back to memories he held dear to his heart; even as he jumped. He knew he had to do this to get back home to Georgia. Then he said, real fast, one to ten. The rip chord had opened up the parachute. He was hovering over the draft of the burning plane. The wind had actually taken charge now. A breeze like angels' wings came and blew him to a clearing. Johnny knew then they were praying back home. Only God could have produced that miracle. He understood his life was no longer in his or the enemies hands. Johnny just assumed that this was it for him. He hoped the other guys landed in safe places and could find one another. So much for getting a letter from Georgia or even home for that matter. Johnny felt something he never felt before. It was as though the very hand of God had created that angelic breeze that had blown his parachute out of the fire draft. Was it the wind or a breath of an angel that swept him out of harm's way? He wondered. That was one hurdle, but there were many more as he landed in the middle of a German camp. It was their anti-craft firing camp. Johnny landed near their blazing campfire.

Immediately a big German soldier grabbed his tags and took a quick look with squinted eyes; he made sure it hurt Johnny's neck. He then put him on a motorcycle with a gun at his back. They drove him through town on display, yelling "War Kriegie!," meaning war prisoners. They then took Johnny to a communal local prison where all the local criminals were held; both men and women. They all shared one big room with wooden slabs and straw for beds along the wall, stacked three high and three wide.

He was told he would be staying there for days until they had collected enough war prisoners to carry them on in the

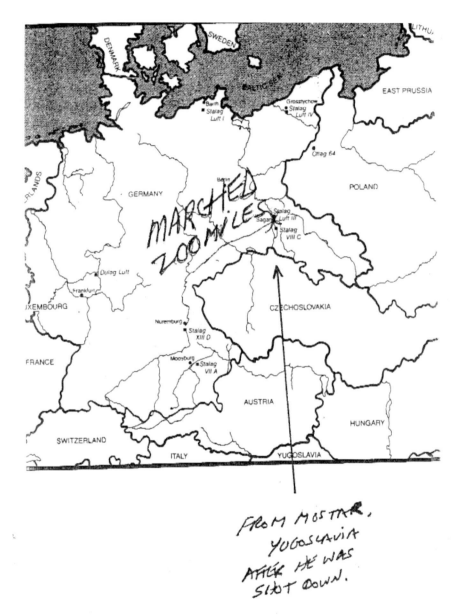

He traveled in a forty by eight train from Mostar, Yugoslavia after he was shot down. Marched 200 miles

1. LAST NAME - FIRST NAME - MIDDLE INITIAL	2. ARMY SERIAL NO.	3. GRADE	4. ARM OR SERVICE	5. COMPONENT
Wiedrich Elmer J	37 555 539	S/Sgt	AC	AUS
6. ORGANIZATION	7. DATE OF SEPARATION		8. PLACE OF SEPARATION	
454th Bomb Gp 739th Bomb Sq	6 Oct 45		AAF Separation Base Santa Ana California	
9. PERMANENT ADDRESS FOR MAILING PURPOSES	10. DATE OF DEATH		11. PLACE OF BIRTH	
Avon Minn	17 Aug 1922		Los Angeles Cal	
12. ADDRESS FROM WHICH EMPLOYMENT WILL BE SOUGHT	13. COLOR EYES	14. COLOR HAIR	15. HEIGHT	16. WEIGHT	17. NO. DEPEND.
Soe 9	Hazel	Brown	5' 9"	165	0
18. RACE	19. MARITAL STATUS	20. U.S. CITIZEN	21. CIVILIAN OCCUPATION AND NO.
X	X		Inspector Materials

MILITARY HISTORY

22. DATE OF INDUCTION	23. DATE OF ENLISTMENT	24. DATE OF ENTRY INTO ACTIVE SERVICE	25. PLACE OF ENTRY INTO SERVICE	
16 Mar 43	25 Mar 43		Fort Snelling Minn	
26.	27. LOCAL S.S. BOARD NO.	28. COUNTY AND STATE	29. HOME ADDRESS AT TIME OF ENTRY INTO SERVICE	
		Stearns Co Minn	Avon Minn	

30. MILITARY OCCUPATIONAL SPECIALTY AND NO.

Airplane Armorer Gunner 612   None

31. BATTLES AND CAMPAIGNS

Air Off Europe   Rome-Arno   Air Combat Balkans

APPLICATION FOR
MINNESOTA
12-41-45

32. DECORATIONS AND CITATIONS

Air Medal   EAME Theat Medal

33. WOUNDS RECEIVED IN ACTION

None

	LATEST IMMUNIZATION DATES				DATE OF DEPARTURE	DESTINATION	DATE OF ARRIVAL
SMALLPOX	TYPHOID	TETANUS	OTHER (specify)				
May 45	31May45	31May45			9 Mar 44	Italy	21 Mar 44
					15 May 45	USA	2 Jun 45
TOTAL LENGTH OF SERVICE		HIGHEST GRADE HELD					
CONTINENTAL SERVICE		FOREIGN SERVICE					
YEARS	MONTHS	DAYS	YEARS	MONTHS	DAYS		
1	3	16	1	2	24	S/Sgt	

39. PRIOR SERVICE

None

40. REASON AND AUTHORITY FOR SEPARATION

AR 615-365 RR1-2 and latter ltr WD Subj: AAF Separation Base dated 6 Sept 1945

41. SERVICE SCHOOLS ATTENDED

Airplane Armorer Lowery Fld Colo Aerial Gunner Las Vegas Nev

PAY DATA

42. LONGEVITY FOR PAY PURPOSES		44. MUSTERING OUT PAY	45.	46. TRAVEL	47. TOTAL AMOUNT, NAME OF DISBURSING OFFICER
YEARS	MONTHS				
2	5	19	100.	1 100.	NONE	112.15	$ 227.75	J. A. MILTON 1T, COL. AC

INSURANCE NOTICE

48. KIND OF INSURANCE	49. HOW PAID	50.					55. INTENTION OF VETERAN
		10 Sep 1945	30 Oct 1945		6.50		

54. REMARKS

Inactive Service ERC 16 Mar 43 to 25 Mar 43
Lapel Button Issued
Adjusted Service Rating 60 (13 Sept 45)

56. SIGNATURE OF PERSON BEING SEPARATED

Elmer J Wiedrich

57. PERSONNEL OFFICER (Type name, grade and organization - signature)

G R Krause 1st Lt A C 1040th AAF BU

Johnny's Honorable Discharge: Very Honorable.

forty and eight train; to be carried into the stark German war prison into the very heart of Germany—if it has a heart at all. He was angry at the politics of war, not the German people, who his bloodline came from. In both prisons he was offered just enough potato soup to stay alive. He slept on a slab of wood with a heap of straw on it that was getting smaller and smaller as it was also his bathroom. When used, that portion had to be shoveled away. Johnny refused to give up. He thought, *My plane ripped into pieces. My crew have had to scatter and all that is left now, literally, is that all encompassing memory of that wonderful girl back home; a girl named Georgia.* They snapped his file out, took his picture, and began interrogation for their reports. In secret, Johnny began his own legal log, documented in a secret code that only he knew, for Washington. He just plain ignored the conditions. He would endure by just holding Georgia in his heart and mind.

The train ride over to Nuremberg prison was no picnic. In fact, it was a copy of the prison he had just left. But it was here, at the Nuremberg prison, one of the German guards yanked at his tags; he gave Johnny a stern and evil look and said, "You German, why you not fight with us? Are you a Chicago gangster?" Johnny looked back in a determined way and replied, "I fight for what is good and what is right and for people to have the right and freedom to be so…not the freedom to do wrong!!!"

The German soldier didn't know English well. He listened for any word or inflection he might understand. He perceived in Johnny's look a determined man to fight against evil. He told a couple of the soldiers to lock him down but that look haunted him; it puzzled him. Just what did it mean to be American?

I'm going to watch this one close. I'm going to find out what makes him tick. What drives a man like this; especially a man who evolved out of our German heritage. What a puzzle. He shook his head.

Letter, letter, letter—that's all Johnny cared about right now; if only there was a letter from her. The prettiest and the smartest girl he had ever known.

The Germans were being driven out of the camp as the Russian bombs were getting too close on the other side of their little camp and town. They were being driven deeper into Germany now by both armies. They had figured out that if they cut off the German's gas and oil supply, the war would be over. So the Americans squeezed off their way and their supplies. *They're good...definitely* good. *But, we're good soldiers, good and prepared,* Johnny thought. They had decided to march the "American Kriegies" over to Stalag seven. It was about seventy miles away, and even though it was dead of winter they were not going to waste anything on them. Gas was definitely short.

As Johnny marched he began to compare those horrific miles over the mountain and trails totally covered with ice and snow to those trapper trails he knew so well in the land of ten thousand lakes. There were plenty of nights he'd felt like he'd done at least one hundred miles. He sure wasn't going home empty, as it meant food for his family and gas for the Model T. Those mink and muskrat furs seem to sell better than anything else.

They had to march day and night with only one small bowl of soup a day—which consisted of a lot of melted snow water and a little barley. They could count the pearls. At night, he and the prisoners would rob the pig sties of their slop and drink the melted snow by day. When they were marched past farms and the others were sleeping, they would dig for frozen potatoes, roots—anything. They would wait for the group leader to fall asleep, even though they knew he was too tired and too old to care; at least he would act as though he didn't see them. *Well, that's not evil,* Johnny thought.

But through it all Johnny kept on course, always toward what he knew was the right thing to do for his country. He never wavered from missing the girl of his dreams.

Each step now was testing every fiber of his being, but he didn't care as long as he could get somewhere to hear from Georgia and to keep his promise to write to her. It seemed he was literally holding on with a bowl of soup and a dream.

The soldiers from the south would get so tired in the march they would lay down in the snow, thinking they would just rest a minute. They would never get back up as they had frozen to death that quick! Johnny tried to get the word to them but they wouldn't listen or maybe they just didn't have anything to hold onto any longer.

Johnny's village had taught him to never stop in the snow. He thought how tired he was when those mink and muskrat had pushed him to the limit, but most of all they taught him not to become the hunted.

Even now, totally surrounded by enemies, man and nature, he knew in his mind how to be free. He could see that was the most important thing! He would have added that to his log, but when his fingers froze, he could no longer hold onto that documented log for Washington. He could sense blisters forming on his feet about the size of half dollars. By now he felt as though he was sleepwalking, but he wasn't going to lie down. He recognized that sleep right now would be a worse enemy than that big old German up front and he thought there was one still in back.

When he saw men falling away, one-by-one, he had saved a little piece of paper to wrap his tags in. He had better take them off now, he thought, while he still could. I'll try to wrap them up in that paper that says "for Georgia." After all, the memory of her was keeping him moving and alive.

He warded off sleep by imagining that beautiful, tall, slender girl back home. She would be running from one of her activities to another one. It seemed like she never slept. He knew she wouldn't rest until everything had been done properly and to the very best of her ability. He never saw Georgia rest!

"Scatter!" rang through his ears like an interloper. They scattered separately into the field trying to find a place to hide. He looked all around and up. They were being shot at by American planes who believed they were the enemy. What an ingenious plan of the Germans; to let the very elite, the strongest survivors who hadn't frozen to death yet die by their own soldiers' hands.

But somehow, on the wings of a prayer and a dream, Johnny did make it to Nuremberg. He was housed in the officer's camp with a library of sorts and a garden. But the miracle of it all was that he could send and receive letters and Red Cross packages. He did receive Georgia's letter with a beautiful picture in it. That letter is still being written today and will go on forever because of Johnny's dogged determination and love for Georgia.

I am including some of Georgia's file of her husband, her soulmate, soldier, warrior, and their family. I hope this true documentary story will make you proud to be an American.

The way to show that pride is the way Johnny did. Love your country, which supports your dreams. Love your family, which supports you, but most of all, love what is right and good. The good Johnny and our soldiers are willing to give their lives for that. In short, love yourself by doing what is right and good!

Johnny never took that seventh step of completion because his story is still going on, forever strong. It will never have an end. I wrote this impression of him. Please read on to see what those who knew him had to say.

The storm has passed like a bird in the night
whose white wings flapped in noisy flight

to bend the willows and flatten reeds
that now stand dripping our wonderful beads.

Once more the pond is calm, serene
take a look through the rain-dark willow screen
take a breath of fresh delightful air
and know forever that I will always be there